GW00729234

THE... STARTS HERE 2009 ...

CAMBRIDGESHIRE

First published in Great Britain in 2009 by
Young Writers, Remus House, Coltsfoot Drive,
Peterborough, PE2 9JX
Tel (01733) 890066 Fax (01733) 313524
All Rights Reserved

© Copyright Contributors 2008
SB ISBN 978-1-84924-110-6

FOREWORD

Young Writers was established in 1990 with the aim of encouraging and nurturing writing skills in young people and giving them the opportunity to see their work in print. By helping them to become more confident and expand their creative skills, we hope our young writers will be encouraged to keep writing as they grow.

Secondary school pupils nationwide have been exercising their minds to create their very own short stories, using no more than fifty words, to be included here in our latest competition *The Adventure Starts Here ... .*

The entries we received showed an impressive level of technical skill and imagination, an absorbing look into the eager minds of our future authors.

CONTENTS

THE MINI SAGAS

THE LOTTERY TICKET

Normal people have money; not me. Every day after school there's children buying sweets. I hate it.

I walk the long way home. As I turn the corner, a gust of wind blows. It stops - something settles to the ground - an unclaimed lottery ticket. Could this be my lucky day?

ISABELLE PEYTON (13)

Bottisham Village College

BATH TIME

The boat tossed and turned in the magnificent storm. Waves like skyscrapers crashed down, knocking the hull to pieces. Wind howled through the torn sail. Then a huge whirlpool opened beneath the boat. A loud, majestic voice called over the storm, 'James, James, bath time's over. I've pulled the plug!'

PENNY WIESER (13)
Bottisham Village College

DINGO TOOK MY BABY

'Who's done it? Any suspects? Where's the baby?'
On Saturday afternoon, the baby disappeared.
Nobody knew anything that had happened. That
day, the baby's clothes were found.
Sunday morning arrived. In the distance they
could hear a baby crying. There were teeth marks
on its neck. What had taken it?

NIKKITA DHARI (13)

Bottisham Village College

THE MONSTER

The spaceship, NASA printed on the side. Blast off!
Landing on Mars. A step out. Cautious and quiet.
Lieutenant Tom and Captain Josh, the first to
Mars. They found their stride using the little
gravity around them. A monster - creeping closer.
Then a tabby cat jumped into the garden.

JENNY SHELLEY (13)
Bottisham Village College

THE CURSE

It's odd the emphasis our tribe puts on age;
being sixteen means everything, then you can
be included. Your spirit is free, you are a Soul
Warrior of the elite guard.
We regretted that rule after Silent Wolf.
Everything changed: harmony evaporated and the
curse infected us all.

KATIE BELLIS (13)
Bottisham Village College

HOMEWORK

There I was. She approached. Oh no! Getting
closer, she'd spotted me! Her warty nose and
yellow, stained teeth. I was so scared! *Buzzz.*
Saved by the buzzer.
Warty nose loomed; she'd have to get my
homework later! 'Charlotte, are you OK?'
(I hadn't done it!) Argh, quick, run!

REBECCA KNOWLES (13)

Bottisham Village College

THE LITTLE HARMLESS TOY CLOWN

A little girl hugs her toy clown tightly. The mechanism within laughs inhumanly. The girl twitches and suddenly the doll moves upwards, reaching out.

Next morning, her mother comes in. A sickening, blood-curdling scream pitches sharply through the house. The toy is broken, smashed, and the girl is dead.

KATIE FRANCE (13)
Bottisham Village College

7

THE STIG

Some say he walked across the desert just to eat a bit of chocolate cake. Rumours have it that he was Asafa Powell in disguise at the Olympics. Jeremy Clarkson has it that he's the fastest on the planet. All we know is he's called The Stig. Cool, calm and perfection.

ALEX LOUGHLAN (13)

Bottisham Village College

THE DIARY OF SIMBA MIWABI

Deep Africa, the jungle. Lion hunting for supper, hiding in the reeds.

'Argh!' I screamed as my foot was bitten off by a huge lion. Then, a bite in the neck and everything went completely black.

Three days later I woke, with no right leg, and still everything was black.

BEN MILLARD (13)

Bottisham Village College

9

A DIARY OF A NORTH AMERICAN SCHOOLGIRL

We got our geography essays back today, wow, I got a Level 8. You could say this was a good thing. It wasn't when Samantha Nicolby found out, she beat me to the floor. I crawled home and fell into the house. Bruises covered my face. Dad phoned school. Uh-oh.

VERITY REEVES (14)

Bottisham Village College

WHAT LIES IN THE SNOW

It was a frosty day in Ducks Wood and the first snowflakes were beginning to fall. Caitlin was out playing with her friends at the park. They were in the snow, when they heard something in a bush. They edged towards it and saw a dead body in the snow.

OLIVIA WAGHORN (13)
Bottisham Village College

11

DROWNING!

I was in the lake and an old man was watching.
I ignored him but when I got out, he walked
over to me. He had something behind him but
I couldn't see what. As I started to run away, he
grabbed my arm and drowned me in the lake.

JAZZMYN TANNER (13)

Bottisham Village College

ALL ALONE

It was dark at Cimbly Wood as I had no light and there was nothing to see or hear. No food or drink. I was left alone with the shining moonlight and the bitter, cold frost piercing my lips and splitting my skin as I lay there all alone.

CONNOR CRAWFORD (13)

Bottisham Village College

UNTITLED

One day there was a little boy and his name was
Billy. He loved school, especially English lessons,
and his teacher was the best in the school.
One day he went to buy his lunch and found he
had no money, so his best mate shared his.

ALISTAIR COOK (13)
Bottisham Village College

THE PHANTOM HOUSE

I was certain that the house was haunted, with all
the noises, creaks and cracks around the house.
Nobody believed me. I had to prove them wrong.
I stayed up all night looking for a way to catch the
phantoms. The bedroom door flung open, but it
was too late …

FAE SEDDON (13)

Bottisham Village College

15

SLEEPLESS NIGHT

I was sleeping in my bed when I woke up because I heard the fire alarm go off. I screamed really loudly, then I realised I couldn't panic. I had a phone in my room. I rang the fire brigade and ran into my mum's room, which was next door.

JESS BYE (14)

Bottisham Village College

THE MAN YOU CANNOT SEE

I sat there in the dark, on my own, looking down
at the gash on my arm, the blood oozing out. I
could hear him breathing as he lashed out again.
That time I screamed. It just made things worse.
He had already killed my parents, what could I
do?

SIÂN TANNER (13)
Bottisham Village College

17

UNTITLED

He hit her. She cowered. Bullets of abuse, each
one more powerful than the last. Distressed
screams echoed from next door. A crash of
porcelain as he shattered her fragile heart. The
cornered child squealed, trapped behind the
ferocious predator.
It was all too much. I changed channel.

MATTHEW BROWN, HUGH BURTON
& CLAIRE HEDGECOTT

Bottisham Village College

IT'S TRUE

When you're asked to make a saga with only fifty words, it's actually quite hard. You start a story and end it a few lines down. It's like an ice cream cone without the ice cream. It's a story with no middle.

But guess what? I did it.

CHRIS BODGER (15)

Bottisham Village College

UNTITLED

The orange glow shone dimly through the ominous fog. The buildings; blocks of concrete, stood - city people of the night. I'd been waiting, wishing, hoping for an age. Then, *click, crack, bang*. He staggered towards me, a mass of plum-purple bruises; scarlet blood. My boyfriend, lying dead in my arms.

KATIE WARD (14)

Bottisham Village College

NOISY ANIMALS

Animals screeching and fighting for the last slice of cake. The noise from outside echoing down the corridors. As one leaves, another enters. The bell calls and the staffroom is once again empty.

KIRSTIE BRAND (14)

Bottisham Village College

SUICIDE

He stood there, wavering, teetering on the
edge of death. The suspension bridge swayed
dangerously, high above the land. A crowd
gathered, shepherded by police. Officials rushed,
scattered below the bridge. A web zipped out of
nowhere. The man
fell …
Then he came, Spider-Man. He swung,
reached out …

TOBY BUTTRESS (14)
Bottisham Village College

WHAT I SAW!

Walking in the park, walking home …
I woke up! Sitting in a chair in *the* room! The big
room! The dark room …
The TV came on, a man on it. 'You're poisoned!
Look up!'
A box.
'That's the antidote … have fun!'
Hands went in. Razor-blades attacked. I was
screwed!

THOMAS ROWLAND

Bottisham Village College

AWAKE

I lay on the table of death. Ravens circled above me. People, supposedly 'healers', cut me open with knives and other weapons. They were supposed to be saving me but this felt like murder. I was paralysed, unable to move a single muscle in my body. I was being operated on, but I was awake!

STEPHANIE FULLER (13)

Bottisham Village College

THE BAD SANTA

Santa was late delivering his presents that night.
He was busy training reindeer so he told Mrs
Claus (his wife) to find someone else to take out
his sleigh. But Santa's replacement caused havoc,
cutting down trees and taking coal to houses
instead. Santa was furious and banished him
forever.

ADAM FISHER (13)

Sir Harry Smith Community College

BANG!

The girl crept into her house. She was confused, she was expecting her mum to be there. Then she saw the trail of blood that was leading round the corner. She crept up to the door; she was leaning against the doorframe. She felt breathing on her neck. *Bang!*

ASHLEY SAVAGE (13)
Sir Harry Smith Community College

DARK NIGHT

The wind is fierce. As it hits you on the cheek it
makes you feel as though you should turn and run
away, but there you stay. The doorway where
you stand creaks under pressure as it threatens to
fall down.
The sun begins to rise; the night's now forgotten.

LAUREN MATTLESS (13)

Sir Harry Smith Community College

WEIRD AND WONDERFUL

We arrived at the picnic area. The sky was dark and the moon was out. It was as if the trees were ganging up on us to kill us. Then, without warning, there were loud bells ringing and reindeer footsteps came nearer. A man got off - he wore red trousers.

ALEX SWEENEY (13)

Sir Harry Smith Community College

THE CURB CRAWLER

I ran and ran as fast as I could. My feet began to ache. I turned back. Shocked, I tripped back. Before me stood a lanky, skinny figure breathing heavily. His screwed-up face dribbled with sweat. In his hand, a knife. He crept towards me. He shouted, 'Die!'

CHARLOTTE JOHNSON (14)
Sir Harry Smith Community College

UNTITLED

A noise downstairs triggered the fear in everyone's faces. A light shone faintly before me, where I picked up a lamp beside my bed and crept to the door. Although Mum didn't want me to go, I did. I reached the bottom of the stairs, where I saw the face …

KATHRYN HARE
Sir Harry Smith Community College

CHRISTMAS MORNING

Christmas morning, at last it was here! I looked at my clock, it was only 5am! I went back to sleep; I'd get up soon.

I woke up again … 8am! I jumped out of bed and rushed downstairs. The room was empty, the front door was open … we'd been robbed!

SAM BOON (13)

Sir Harry Smith Community College

NIGHT COMBAT

He walked endlessly through the dark of night,
trying to find respite from the incessant rattle
of gunfire. Then all of a sudden, *bang!* The
ground shuddered beneath his battered feet.
Light glistened before him. He began to panic,
trembling from head to toe. Could this really be
the end?

SAM KILLINGWORTH (13)

Sir Harry Smith Community College

SOMEWHERE

Somewhere to hide. Where? Cupboard? No, too
obvious. Footsteps coming. Quick. Where? Got
it. Under the bed I crawl. Louder and louder the
footsteps come. All I do is wait. Will he find me?
the door is open, I see his shoes.
'Come out!'
He finds. He hits. He hurts.

NICOLA CRANWELL (14)
Sir Harry Smith Community College

THE BAD CONDUCTOR

Once, a bus conductor murdered his passengers.
He was sent to the electric chair.
First he ate a banana and the chair wouldn't
electrocute him. He did this the next day and the
day after. Someone asked him, 'How do bananas
stop you dying?'
'They don't; I'm just a bad conductor!'

JAMES DIETZ (13)

Sir Harry Smith Community College

THE NOISE!

A terrible noise woke him; it was coming from outside. He crept downstairs. As he went, the noise grew louder and harsher in his ears. He got downstairs and glanced at the clock; it was ten o'clock. He went to the door and opened it as he thought ... *carol-singers*.

JACOB BEEBE (13)
Sir Harry Smith Community College

CHRISTMAS NIGHT NOISES

I wake. *What's the time? Five.* I have a whole
three hours to wait. *Crash! What is that?* Getting
out of bed, I creep downstairs, there's presents
everywhere. I crept towards my pile.
'What are you doing, boy?'
Fear grips me. Turning, I see the biggest ever
belly. Santa's belly!

DOM FRADLEY (13)
Sir Harry Smith Community College

UNTITLED

It was midnight and I awoke. I was shivering all over. I went to put the heating on. It was pitch-black and I couldn't see anything. I heard a creak coming from behind me. I turned around and the last thing I remembered was a dagger coming at me.

CHARLOTTE SAVIDGE
Sir Harry Smith Community College

THE PEOPLE AT THE DOOR

She unlocked the door and entered her freezing house. She threw her keys on the sofa, whilst tying up her hair.
Ding-dong. She walked towards the door and slowly opened it. Three boys stood covered in blood, staring at her.
'Trick or treat,' they yelled, smiling at the girl.

MEGAN FIDLER (13)
Sir Harry Smith Community College

CHRISTMAS EVE

Bang! 'Ow!' I rushed downstairs and there he was in the fireplace. Santa Claus! He was all covered in soot. After a moment he got up and started greedily eating mince pies and gulping down the sherry. He put some presents under the tree, while I went back to bed.

MEGAN LANE (13)

Sir Harry Smith Community College

HALLOWE'EN CREEPS

One scary night, Jack was wandering the town on Hallowe'en at 7pm. He was supposed to meet Luis, his big brother. Jack heard footsteps, three, then stop. *Clack, clack, clack,* they went. Jack ran! 'Come back!' they shouted. A young voice, male. 'Hey, it's me,' Luis said. 'Like my shoes?'

EMELIE VARDON (14)

Sir Harry Smith Community College

CHRISTMAS MORNING

I awoke early that morning. I crept downstairs to see what was under our Christmas tree and, to my surprise, there was a small package moving. I walked over to it and I opened it, and there was a brand new puppy staring back at me. I was so happy.

PATRICIA GLETHEROW (14)

Sir Harry Smith Community College

SANTA

As I began to drift to sleep on Christmas Eve,
I was suddenly awoken when I heard thudding
downstairs. I went to investigate, to find Santa in
a bright red suit, and a sack of presents at the foot
of the chimney.
'I'll take this carrot for Rudolph,' he smiled.

ANOUSHKA ADAM (13)
Sir Harry Smith Community College

WHO'S THAT MAN?

I woke up with a start. I could hear a noise. I climbed out of bed and walked towards the door. There was a bright light downstairs. There were voices. I walked out into the hallway. I could see someone coming up the stairs. Facing me was a bearded man …

ASHLEIGH WHITWELL
Sir Harry Smith Community College

LAST DUNE

'Twas midday. Nelson Mandela had escaped from prison. He had no water and was about to give up, when he heard music. He climbed the sand dune and was amazed at the sight of thousands of monkeys dancing The Macarena. Hallucination? He joined in and was eaten alive.

RYAN ELLINGTON (12)
Sir Harry Smith Community College

WHO'S THERE?

My birthday, full of joy and light, or so I thought.
I woke up, rustling sounds haunted the area
around. Black was everywhere. Floorboards
creaked as I crept downstairs. A light was on.
I grabbed a pan and started to creep into the
room. Nobody was around.
Suddenly, 'Surprise!'

SIANA RAWLINGS (12)

Sir Harry Smith Community College

OUT OF THE ASHES - A RE-TELLING OF THE BOOK

My great life, young Josh is born and the cows are milking well. It could not be better.
On the news, foot and mouth hits Scotland … then the farm which is ten miles away. Sadly, it's hit us. Dad has become ill.
What will happen next? Good or bad news?

LOUISE LINDSEY (12)
Sir Harry Smith Community College

DAY BY DAY

The hungry eyes darted around the room for something else to look at. The fingers tapped angrily against the desk in utter impatience. Feet scraped across the carpet, bored of being confined to the same area. The minutes dragged like hours as pupils restlessly awaited the end of the day.

EMILY HALL (13)

Sir Harry Smith Community College

YOUR MISSION

Sixteen-year-old Bob finds himself in a secret
organization set up by highly-trained agents. His
mission is to find a UFO. In America he finds it
and an epic mind battle begins. The alien has a
strong mind and crushes Bob to a pulp.
Aliens will always prevail.

THOMAS BAXTER (13)

Sir Harry Smith Community College

VAMPIRE SAVES A LIFE

Steve was walking home. He was approached
by a mysterious man who gave him two tickets
to a freak show. He took Darren as well. Steve
wanted to become a vampire but couldn't.
Darren stole a vampire's spider. It bit Steve.
Darren transformed into a vampire to save
Steve's life!

PAISLEY CORLEY (12)
Sir Harry Smith Community College

ERAGON

Long ago, in the land of Alagaesia, young Eragon
finds an egg. The egg hatches; it's a dragon named
Saphira. Uncle Garrow dies and Eragon vows to
kill the murdering Ra-Zac. They reach the Varden,
who help them defeat Shade Durza, but nothing's
as it seems. Will he die?

THOMAS SMITH (12)
Sir Harry Smith Community College

BEHIND THE GATES!

We drove up the lane and suddenly saw the old house behind the big iron gates. Something drew me to that house. As I approached, a figure appeared at the door. A man with a familiar face was in front of me. glancing at the photos, I recognised my grandad.

RACHEL RUSH (12)

Sir Harry Smith Community College

FLOATING AWAY

Around the sacred waterhole of Zambia, the tribe
was gathering, worshipping.
High above, 'Whisky, Alfa, Tango, Echo, Romeo.'
A container scooped down from the fire
helicopter and emptied the hole.
Suddenly, the tribe floated upwards, their heads
like balloons filled with anger, expanded, and they
followed their sacred water.

ALEX FORREST (13)

Sir Harry Smith Community College

UNTITLED

He ran through the jungle, spears flying at him. He was in Australia. He couldn't believe he had stolen the chest that was lost 1,000 years ago. A spear flew through the green leaves and brown bark. It caught his arm.
'Cut, good scene. Change rolls. Ready and *action!*'

DANIEL BARSBY (13)

Sir Harry Smith Community College

UNTITLED

I awoke with a start, only to find Santa Claus standing before me, holding lots of presents. He looked shocked, dropped the presents and disappeared into thin air. I had just seen him! Santa! I wondered where he was going now? I wondered if I was just dreaming.

JODI-ANN HARRY (14)

Sir Harry Smith Community College

WILL I DROWN?

The water was dripping. It was going faster and
faster; getting deeper and deeper. The *whoosh* of
the water echoed everywhere. All I could hear
was the waves moving; the water filling my ears
up. Finally, a loud boom ...
Then Mum shouted, 'Turn your bath water off!'

CHARLOTTE COX (14)

Sir Harry Smith Community College

WATER

Looking around, I saw a shark swimming right towards me, turning at the last minute. Fish surrounded me. In the water everything looked different, or was that my glasses?
Mum called me. 'Aquarium, cool! Glad we came?'
'Definitely, Mum!'
We walked out of the sealife sanctuary with a smile.

HANNAH MEPHAM (13)
Sir Harry Smith Community College

CHRISTMAS

They fly around at Christmas, they have tiny
wings. They help out Santa or at least they try,
but always end up causing trouble. They've got
little pots of magic dust which they sprinkle
everywhere. What mischief they cause. They're
so tiny, like a dot. They're the troublesome
Christmas fairies.

KIRA GRIFFITHS (13)

Sir Harry Smith Community College

WHAT'S FOR DINNER?

The little girl entered the kitchen with her friend.
'Who's this?' her mother asked.
'My friend, I've brought her for dinner,' she
replied.
The mother's face turned to a greedy grin. The
friend looked quite frightened now. The girl
looked at her.
'Throw her in the oven then!' Mother said.

MELISSA WARD (13)
Sir Harry Smith Community College

THE UNKNOWN SURPRISE!

She crept into the dark castle. Screams filled the hallowed halls, making her spine tingle. It soon went silent, with her heart beating faster than ever. Reaching the end of the hall, she opened the door. Suddenly …'Surprise! Happy birthday!' The lights switched on, smiles loomed happily all around her.

EMILY SAVAGE (13)
Sir Harry Smith Community College

THE CHRISTMAS I'LL NEVER FORGET

Snow is falling. It's that time of year again. I put up the Christmas tree with the decorations. It's time to go out as I have to do the Christmas shopping. Busy streets covered in snow as I walk to the shop. I can't get in. Why can't I?

AMBER KENNY (13)
Sir Harry Smith Community College

EMPTY BOXES

I run downstairs. It's Christmas Day. Our tree is surrounded by presents. All for me. I open them one after the other; box after box after box. All empty. Why are they all empty? I turn round. Mum and Dad are stood at the door, arms full of presents!

LUCY WATTS (13)
Sir Harry Smith Community College

MYSTERY VISITOR

It was late and it was dark. I was in the house on my own. I was scared. The door rattled and shrieked. Why did it always happen to me? The door opened further and a hand peered round the door. It opened further. Someone entered my house. But who?

ALICE BAILEY (13)

Sir Harry Smith Community College

CHRISTMAS DAY!

I quickly ran downstairs, eager to open all my presents. I opened the door to the living room. There was the big Christmas tree, but underneath it there was nothing! Where were the presents? I turned around to see Mum with lots of gifts in her hands.
'Merry Christmas!'

CLARISE CARRINGTON (13)

Sir Harry Smith Community College

DÉJÀ VU

I was about to start a new school. I went in and knew where all my classrooms were and what my homework was.

I went home that night and lay awake, wondering why this was happening to me. Should I tell Mum or not? I believe I am going mad.

SAFFRON RUSSELL (13)

Sir Harry Smith Community College

FURY OF THE WAR

It has been a long time since it started. There have been many ferocious attacks. We have lost many loved ones. Life is difficult in the trenches. We write to our families telling them lies about how good it is. We can't tell them the truth.

BROOKLAND SAVAGE (13)
Sir Harry Smith Community College

ALIENS MAKE THE WORLD SPIN ROUND!

On one foggy morning, I was walking down an abandoned road. I suddenly froze. I saw an army of spaceships in the sky and they all had giant magnets. The Earth moved to the right, although it seemed to stop. I felt unsteady. I looked up, nothing was there!

JOSHUA KINSEY (11)

Sir Harry Smith Community College

THE LOCKERS

Suzie walked towards the lockers. The door
slammed behind her. It was very dark, very dark.
She heard heavy breathing. She felt like she was
being watched. The last sound that was heard
was her loud, high-pitched scream.

NAOMI HALL (11)
Sir Harry Smith Community College

AFRICAN MADNESS

I was stuck in Africa. All of a sudden there was
a noise. As it got closer, it got louder. It was
elephants. 'Is this a dream?' I said.
When it was over there was a mess. Nobody was
there. I walked for miles until I came across a lion.

AARON DUNMORE (11)
Sir Harry Smith Community College

DEAD RED HOOD

'Now go to your grandma's,' her mother said as she kicked Little Red's gluteus maximus so hard she flew through the air, over the forest and straight into a big wolf's mouth and was eaten.

JACOB MCADIE (12)
Sir Harry Smith Community College

OUT OF THIS WORLD!

We landed on the moon. When we got out, we felt eerie darkness around us. Egg-like creatures with hamsters running in their heads hovered towards us. As they drew closer, loud party music began to play. The aliens were sucked off the face of the moon, but what by?

MEGAN BAILEY (12)
Sir Harry Smith Community College

OH NO! CAPTURED!

I was walking in the jungle when a bag was put
over my head. I was then in a boat. I felt ill.
I arrived in America and got on a boat to England.
I performed and was sold to the circus. My show
is called, 'The Amazing Monkey'.

NATASHA BROUGH (14)

Sir Harry Smith Community College

71

DEAR DIARY

17th July.
What happened in the last 24 hours I'm hoping is a nightmare. It was my fault. I will never be able to forgive myself. He's fighting for his life because of me.
17th August.
He's finally home. The guilt has gone. I will never make that mistake again.

CARLY LEFEVRE (13)

Sir Harry Smith Community College

STEVEN HAWKINS IS KIDNAPPED

It's World War III and the year is 3002, and Group Alpha have had to go back in time to the year 2008 to kidnap Steven Hawkins for his ideas for doomsday devices. His ideas would help greatly in the war. With his intellect and their engineering skills, they'll win.

MARTYN EVERDEN (13)

Sir Harry Smith Community College

73

MY AFRICAN ADVENTURE

Dear Diary, it's coming to the end of my first day in Africa. I'm not missing my friends yet, but I'm sure I will soon. I haven't been eaten by lions or bitten by snakes, but I'm still quite scared. Maybe I shouldn't visit the zoo again for a while.

SOPHIE BROUGHTON (14)
Sir Harry Smith Community College

THE LAKE

'Ouch!' cried Bridget. 'What's going on?'
'We're going in,' called the driver.
Suddenly, *splash,* and they were in the lake.
How could things get any worse? thought Bridget.
She didn't even want to come.
'We're going to drown,' shouted an old woman.
Five minutes later …
'Ride's ended,' shouted the driver.

ELEANOR EATON (13)
Sir Harry Smith Community College

75

DARK WATERS

She walks up the stairs; it's dark. Up one flight,
up another, not a sound to be heard apart from
the clonk of her feet. She stands at the top of the
stairs. She slips. She falls, sliding left and right,
then *splash!*
Now, wasn't that a fun water slide!

LAURA PETTIT (14)

Sir Harry Smith Community College

IN THE JUNGLE!

It was sunny in Africa. Lenny Lion and Gary Giraffe found a mysterious creature - a human! The human spoke quietly, a shocked look on her face as the animals danced. Suddenly, rain began to fall. They performed their own version of 'Singing in the Rain'. They then ate the human!

AIMEE JEPSON (14)
Sir Harry Smith Community College

STICKY CHRISTMAS

It was Christmas Eve. However, Santa thought it was Easter, so he crept into the house and left some eggs under the tree.
The next morning, Brian woke up. All the eggs were melted under the tree. Brian put his foot in the chocolate and got stuck for evermore.

EMMA ROBINETT (14)

Sir Harry Smith Community College

HEARTBROKEN

Dear Diary, so warm, but so cold out here in
Lapland. It's my birthday, I'm gonna be sixteen.
Dear Diary, I'm so sad. Even though it's my
birthday, my heart's in two. He's mean. He
couldn't even say it to my face. I'm so angry.
Please, please help me, Mummy.

SOPHIE RIMES (13)
Sir Harry Smith Community College

ALL A DREAM?

Sarah wakes up to find three ghostly figures taking her hand. They lead her out through the window and fly across the town. They give Sarah a locket and tell her to remember them.
She wakes up - it was all a dream. Then she sees the locket on her pillow.

EMILY POLSON (13)

Sir Harry Smith Community College

THE PLANNED ESCAPE

'I'm not going to that school. You've dragged me
here against my will. Let me have some freedom,'
I screamed at her.
'Lola, you are going to that school if you like it or
not,' screamed Mum.
I've got to get out of this country, and fast.

EMILY BEEBY (13)
Sir Harry Smith Community College

A STABLE

The hostages' safety was the priority. The SAS team made their way through the jungle. They fired a couple of rounds at the terrorists. They ran towards the hostages, just to find Mary and Joseph with Baby Jesus and a donkey.

OLIVER LONG (13)
Sir Harry Smith Community College

THE DARKNESS IS COMING

The darkness is coming, it's all around. The
darkness is coming, will you be found? The
darkness is coming, say goodbye to the light. The
darkness is coming, can you fight?
That was when my mum turned off my television.

SAMUEL POWELL (14)
Sir Harry Smith Community College

DOG, THE STUNTMAN

My name's Dog, I'm a dog and I'm gonna try a stunt.
'OK, you're good to go.'
I ran forward, jumped onto the trampoline and bounced onto the roof. I had done it, I was on the roof, but I didn't realise I had to get back down!

REECE GORDON (13)
Sir Harry Smith Community College

THE STALKER

On a cold December night, Sally Jenkins was walking home from work, her footsteps echoing down the alley. The stranger approached from behind, keeping to the shadows. Sally felt like she was being watched. The stranger was catching up. He tapped her on the back. 'Save £39 with the RAC.'

AARON HALL (13)

Sir Harry Smith Community College

ALONE

Melissa looked around. She heard creaking noises.
She was not alone! She ran up the stairs towards
her bedroom but it was locked. She turned to
the bathroom. She opened the door and ran in.
Frightened and scared, she sat on the floor hoping
that nothing was there. Then *bang!*

ALICE SAVAGE (11)
Sir Harry Smith Community College

THE GHOST

She walked into the pitch-black house and opened the door. A huge white ghost flew out. She screamed. The ghost picked her up and flew away never to be seen again.
Her parents looked for her every day but always had no luck. They never saw her ever again.

CHLOE BAVISTER (11)
Sir Harry Smith Community College

THE SHOCK OF MY LIFE

It was cold, dark and worst of all, down an alley. I was coming back from a party. I heard footsteps coming round the corner. My body froze with fear. Then it came round the corner. I wondered what I was worrying about. 'Hi Lucy,' I called.

MATTHEW ANDREW (12)
Sir Harry Smith Community College

DINOSAUR MAYHEM

Dinosaurs stared down at me, a Triceratops to my left and T-rex to my right. It was dark, so dark I could barely see the cobblestone floor. A door came into view. Suddenly a man with a flashlight appeared. He said, 'Sorry, this museum is closed.'

HANNAH POPE (11)
Sir Harry Smith Community College

HORRIFYING HORROR

It was dark, noisy and terrifying. There was screaming coming from all directions. As his head got chopped off, my stomach churned. I screamed and reached under my chair. I tensely picked a box up and reached in, grabbing some popcorn and carried on watching the movie.

KIMBERLEY WIDNALL (11)

Sir Harry Smith Community College

THE DOG FIGHT

I was in my Spitfire, I could see the German
planes coming towards me. I knew what to
do and I was ready for them. The one coming
towards me I would battle. Hopefully I would kill
him. I went upwards, turned and fired. He spun
towards the cliff. *Dead!*

JOSHUA FOWLER (11)
Sir Harry Smith Community College

WHAT THE LION HAD FOR LUNCH

Mercedes and her family are on safari in Africa.
They see elephants, giraffes and lions. Mercedes
thinks the lions are beautiful. 'Can we go out and
look at the lions close up?' asks Mercedes.
They get out of the truck. Mercedes gets eaten.
The lion licks its lips. 'Yum-yum.'

NADINE EVERETT (11)
Sir Harry Smith Community College

SUZANNE: THE UNNECESSARY HEROINE

The fire bell screeched. Suzanne filled with panic as she lost her way through the screaming children. Then, as if by magic, she caught sight of the fire escape door. As Suzanne burst open the doors in triumph the head teacher, Mr Winfrey, announced, 'It was only a practice!'

TONI FREEMAN (12)
Sir Harry Smith Community College

THE ZEBRA AND BABY

Zooloo, the zebra, found a chubby baby so she took it home.
The next day, Zooloo went to see it. He was missing. Zooloo searched everywhere to find him and she caught a glimpse of him hiding in a tree. She snatched him and carried on her life more carefully.

EMMALISE COLE (11)

Sir Harry Smith Community College

THE HOUSE

Ronald opened his eyes. In front of him was
a scary, menacing house with lighting flashing
behind it. How frightening! 'Argh!' he exclaimed,
falling backwards. Upon looking up again,
however, he chuckled. 'Silly me!' he laughed in his
Australian accent. 'Must have fallen asleep in front
of the television!'

JACOB HARRIS (12)
Sir Harry Smith Community College

THE BANK

Not seeing that it was closed, James walked into
the City Bank, but to his horror, the sight that
greeted him was two gunmen demanding cash.
Afraid, he put his hands up.
Suddenly, a voice. 'Cut! Who's that?'
The gunmen stopped. Only then did James see
the director's chair.

JACK HARRIS (12)

Sir Harry Smith Community College

THE A-TEAM

In America, the A-Team were on the trail. Adam, Ash, Aaron, Amanda and Amber searched the house. They heard eight clicks, then Ash started to scream. The others watched as Ash was sucked into nothingness by a green man with horns and a sucker to eat people in seconds!

ADAM STANLEY (11)
Sir Harry Smith Community College

97

JUST A BIKE RIDE

School had finished and I would be on my way home, but a man had stolen my bag. I jumped on my bike and started to chase him. When I was next to the man, I grabbed my bag. Then I went home and acted like nothing had happened.

BRADLEY MOORES (12)

Sir Harry Smith Community College

MY TRIP TO SOUTH AMERICA

Today we're travelling to South America. We are going to try and live in an Amish culture. It feels really weird. Me and my brother can't live without the TVs and laptop.
I have made an Amish friend, she is really nice. I hope we can stay friends.

KAYLEIGH WHITE (12)

Sir Harry Smith Community College

RUN!

It was a wet, windy day. Tammy was walking home from school. She kept looking back, hearing creaking noises. She wasn't alone. The noise was getting louder and louder. She was miles from home; she didn't know what to do. She looked back. *Run!*

CHARLEY IRELAND (11)

Sir Harry Smith Community College

MY TREK THROUGH NORTH AMERICA

As I walked through the cold towns of North America, I came across some giant bears. I ran as fast as I could. Then I came across a gigantic building which I ran into and slammed the door. The bear came to the door looking for some food.

JACK CORNEY (11)

Sir Harry Smith Community College

MISSION

There were two brothers called Luke and Cameron. They went to Australia to fight for the SAS to make an outbreak. They went to break out Marie and Marcus. They got into the Ford F-150 4x4 and tried to escape. There was a big fight with guns and cars.

LUKE GITTINS (11)
Sir Harry Smith Community College

THE MONSTER

Max was walking down the stairs when he heard a crunch. He looked down; there was a giant monster there. He ran down the stairs and ran for the door but the monster got him. He was about to eat Max when he hit the monster on the nose.

SEAN CLIFFORD (11)
Sir Harry Smith Community College

WAR IN ASIA

As I jumped out of the aeroplane, I kept thinking, *how will we kill their leader?* There were only six of us. We were the best. We ran straight through the jungle, killing people as we went. On our radar, a herd of enemy were coming. We were dead.

LEVI BOISTER (12)

Sir Harry Smith Community College

2005 CHAMPIONS LEAGUE FINAL

On the 25th May, Liverpool played AC Milan in the Champions League Final at Istanbul. When the game had started, straight away AC Milan had scored. Before I knew it, they were 3-0 up at half-time. Then Liverpool came back to make it 3-3. Liverpool won with penalties.

ADAM JEPSON (11)
Sir Harry Smith Community College

UNTITLED

I was in English yesterday and there were boys
messing around, and the teacher caught them.
As people were talking, Belinda walked in and
came to sit next to me. As she was coming over,
I stared. Then she asked, 'Do you want to be
friends?'

MELISSA PETERS (12)

Sir Harry Smith Community College

IT WASN'T SO SCARY AFTER ALL

I went to see my dog that I had adopted. I arrived, I stepped inside. It was cold and dark. I walked in. The door creaked, the light turned on. There was my dog. It ran up and licked me. I expected something else. Not so bad after all!

ZOE BAXTER (12)

Sir Harry Smith Community College

DEAR DIARY

'Captain's log: Things are looking grim, morale's
at an all-time low. The ship's hands are no longer
stimulated by coffee; because there is none.
Just the fact that me being away from the wheel
strikes fear! They don't say it - I can tell.'
That was my final entry before …

JACK MOSELEY-HUTCHINSON (12)

Sir Harry Smith Community College

THE DAY I SLIPPED OVER MY BOAT!

At 7pm on Friday, 13th, I slipped over my Topper boat. There was ice at the bottom, ice at the top, ice on the sail and ice on the chicken! I stepped over the hull, stepped in the bottom and fell head first. That was the day I slipped over.

EDWARD ASHWORTH (12)

Sir Harry Smith Community College

109

A FEW MORE STEPS

The door slammed. She took a few steps. The floorboard creaked. She took a few more steps. The window smashed. She took a few more steps. The wolves howled. She took a few more steps. A hand appeared on her shoulder. Oh no, she never took a few more steps.

ARRON SURRIDGE-TAYLOR (12)

Sir Harry Smith Community College

THE DAY I ROBBED A BANK

I walk in normally. I am next in the queue. Here it goes. I pulled the gun from my pocket and I scream for the money. They hand it over and I sprint for the door. This is the day I managed to rob a bank with a BB gun.

THOMAS PHILLIPS (12)
Sir Harry Smith Community College

THE HAUNTED HOUSE

I walked up to the gate. I gulped. My hand was trembling as I took hold of the handle. It creaked open. I stepped in. The gate slammed shut like a crocodile's mouth. There were gravestones everywhere. I started to run. Someone was shouting me, but who? *Bang!*

SOPHIE SMITH (13)

Sir Harry Smith Community College

SANTA'S TALE

Once there was a man called Fred Claus. He was the saint of Christmas, he brought presents to everyone. He was a lonely man; he only ever got noticed at Christmas. He felt special. For once he had people on his side and there were cheerful people singing again.

KEELAN COCHRANE (13)

Sir Harry Smith Community College

A NIGHT WITH ... IT

She curled up waiting for it. The door opened, creaking. She felt all of the hairs on her back stand up; a shiver down her spine. Waiting, waiting ... how could it be so silent? She longed for a comforting noise, something to make her not feel so alone with it.

MEGAN SAUNDERS (12)
Sir Harry Smith Community College

VERY, VERY, VERY

It was a very, very, very, very, very cold and miserable day. It made me very, very, very, very, very upset. I walked into the house and it was very, very, very, very, very warm. I went and sat in front of the fire with my dog and fell asleep.

FRANKIE HUNTER (13)

Sir Harry Smith Community College

UNTITLED

Monday. Dear Diary, my friends hate me.
Tuesday. Dear Diary, my friends hit me.
Wednesday. Dear Diary, my friends swear at me.
Thursday. Dear Diary, I hate myself. I want to kill
myself.
Friday. Dear Diary, *dead!*

MAIYA GREENWOOD

Sir Harry Smith Community College

MARRY ME!

We sat by the river. I glared into his big brown eyes. the sun was glaring down on us. A beautiful dove flew and sat next to us. We strolled towards the sunset hand in hand. He fell to the floor and pulled out a ring. 'Marry me!'

CHARLOTTE CROWLEY (13)

Sir Harry Smith Community College

MY FRIEND, I MISS YOU

Here in my heart is your name. I miss you. You
were my best friend. Why did you have to go?
The tears and the laughter and avoiding disaster.
The laughs and the twinkle in your eyes. A bullet
ruined your life and mine too. My friend, I miss
you.

MWABA CHIMBA (12)

Sir Harry Smith Community College

I MISS YOU

I miss you. I miss your smile. I miss you. I miss
your laugh. I miss you. I miss your kind words. I
miss you. I miss your comforting ways. I miss you.
I miss your pretty face. I miss you. Where did you
go? Mummy, I miss you.

LUCY JAKES (13)

Sir Harry Smith Community College

119

MY BEST FRIEND

We do everything together. She's my best friend. I can tell her anything. She's my best friend. She's there for me no matter what. She's my best friend. Always there to wipe away my tears. She's my best friend. To catch me when I fall. She's my best friend … *always!*

KIRSTEN OGLESBY (13)

Sir Harry Smith Community College

DOCTOR WHO: WHERE DID I LEAVE IT?

The Doctor ran frantically around the TARDIS
setting the controls. Where was it? Where's his
sonic screwdriver? He'd searched the Elizabethan
times, and almost got his head chopped off. To
Victorian times, he'd been mugged! Where was it?
This was driving him mad!
He reached into his pocket. 'Oops!'

TORI BOS (13)

Sir Harry Smith Community College

STAYED

The wind whistled through the crack in the window. Dad was beating Mum again and if I was to go downstairs, I would get a beating, so I stayed. The screams hurt.
I suddenly woke up. If only I had gone downstairs maybe Mum would be alive.

KERRI PURCELL (12)
Sir Harry Smith Community College

THE HOUSE

I walked to the door; silence. The door opened;
silence. I went into the kitchen and standing there
was a man with blood dripping from his fingers!
I ran as fast as I could but the door was shut. I
screamed. He'd come from the farm with a baby
lamb.

JOY SAWYN (12)

Sir Harry Smith Community College

EVACUATION

It's 1949. I left home today. Mother was so upset,
so was I. Anyway, I am writing this from a big,
posh manor house. The only problem is that
I have to work as a servant. I've already made
them breakfast.
Oh well, at least I won't get blown up …

LAUREN GREENSMITH (13)

Sir Harry Smith Community College

WHAT IS THAT!

One dark, miserable day in the Christmas
holidays, Eleanor lay in her bed thinking. Suddenly
she heard a creak. She shouted, 'Hello?' No one
answered. She got out of bed, opened the door,
slowly. She went downstairs. It was a mouse. She
screamed with laughter. 'I'm such a silly girl.'

EMILY HILL (12)
Sir Harry Smith Community College

EPISODE 7: TIME TO DIE (STAR WARS)

It was a dusty morning on Naboo. Luke was wandering around, then out of the corner of his eye he saw something crashing on Naboo! He rushed over and saw Darth Sidious. He took out his lightsaber and battled. Luke's arm got sliced off, but then he killed Darth Sidious!

BEN MUCKLIN (13)

Sir Harry Smith Community College

RONALDO VS ROBINHO

It was a sunny Thursday evening. Ronaldo and Robinho were having a kick-up competition. Oh, and would you look at this skill. Ronaldo's winning so far, but Ronaldo just kicked the ball as high as he can and it just hit him on the head and knocked him out!

AARON WARRENER (13)

Sir Harry Smith Community College

LOVE

I loved you but you cheated on me. You made me
feel special and you made me feel happy. I could
never know why you did this to me. I'm sorry I
could never be all you wanted. Now I'm happy.
I'm happy I left this abusive relationship.

TAMARA TEMBO (13)
Sir Harry Smith Community College

THE BLACK BEAST

It's dawn. The moon is bright, full and deadly. Any moment the dark, devious beast shall burst through the door, snarling as it comes. With its blood-red eyes that scare a man's soul and its wolf-like features: teeth, fur, razor claws, jagged muscularity. *Gasp ... thud ... thud ... thud ... bang!*

DOMINIC LAMBERT (14)

Sir Harry Smith Community College

THE DAY OF DARKNESS

Kelly hated life. There were rumours and lies spread around. She wanted to disappear. She had lots of meetings with teachers, they didn't help. Kelly moved schools for a fresh start. Everything turned out fresh. She made new friends and was happy for evermore.

EMILY SKEELS (14)
Sir Harry Smith Community College

THE MYSTERIOUS OLD LADY

As I walked down the long, dark alley, there in
the distance I saw a house I'd never seen before.
It was tall and had iron gates. I heard an owl hoot
and realised it was getting dark. I turned around.
Someone grabbed my ear.
'Help!' I cried. Nothing happened.

CARLY WORLDING (13)

Sir Harry Smith Community College

THE CAVE

Tim and Dom went out. They discovered a
dark and gloomy cave. They went to see what
was inside. They heard strange noises and saw
movement inside. They saw a glowing object in
the distance. Dom picked it up; it was gold. Tim
celebrated and woke all the bats. *Argh!*

RYAN TRINCI (13)

Sir Harry Smith Community College

THE GIRL IN THE NIGHT

The girl in the night comes out every full moon.
She's as fast as a cheetah, as sly as a burglar. She
goes in your house and steals your food. She's out
the house before you can say, 'Stop.' She's the girl
in the night who gives you a fright.

BRADLEY STEPHENS (14)
Sir Harry Smith Community College

THE TRUTH OR LIES

Sally was sad. Her dad said her hamster had died, but then she found him. She was doing the hoovering and she had to clean out the Hoover, when she saw a tail. She pulled the tail, she pulled it to see her small hamster in the Hoover bag.

DANIELLE HUNT (13)
Sir Harry Smith Community College

THE UNKNOWN MONSTER

Walking through Funnel Avenue was when I heard
it: a loud growl coming from the darkness. I stood
still. Thundering out of the darkness, it pounced.
I got out of its grasp and sprinted. Problem:
where was my house? The thing behind me, and
nowhere to hide, I was *doomed!*

SEAN WARD (12)

Soham Village College

WHAT WAS THAT?

It was getting dark and misty. I was walking through the slushy snow home. What was that? Something enormous was watching me. I was about to run when something loudly howled. My heart raced. It looked angry. I felt sick. Slowly, I shuffled towards ... the snowman!

SOPHIE JAGGARD (11)

Soham Village College

SEPARATION

I wasn't there and nor was he. I died but he lived.
I hated and he loved. We were all different but no
one cared. My corpse was cremated but he lived
to be a billionaire.
Morose and compassionate would not combine,
so I went to Hell. Without my twin.

ARTHUR FERNANDES (11)

Soham Village College

THE RUNAWAY RAT

Strolling home in the dark, something was behind me. I turned. What was it? I was unaided, no one around, just me. There was a ghostly silence. I started to scurry, but fell. Hot breath on my neck, eyes swollen and a wiry tail … teeth baring. The sly fox!

GRACIE JANE BEYNON (11)

Soham Village College

THE JOURNEY TO THE PARK

Walking to the park at 4pm, I felt something was wrong. I walked straight past the park! I ran as fast as I could, then I came to a dead end! What should I do? Run? Scream? I turned around and that was when I saw ... *Argh!*

CHLOE VAIL (12)

Soham Village College

DON'T LOOK NOW

Dark, scared, my head filled with horror as I dreaded what would come next. I walked down the narrow path, my heart pounding at the speed of light, when suddenly there it was, its eyes red with anger, steam coming from each ear. It was … *my teacher!*

CLARICE SPRUCE (11)

Soham Village College

DROWNED?

I had been in the water for hours, icy-cold, tired.
Sharks were swimming beneath me and any
moment I would feel the snap of jaws around my
feet.

The next thing I knew I was on my back and
everything around me was shining. Where was I?
Was I ... dead?

JEMIMAH THOMPSON (11)

Soham Village College

TRAPPED

Racing through the woods towards me, as fast as
light. I screamed wildly as I ran for my life but it
was hopeless. I was in the middle of nowhere, not
a soul could hear me. I knew I couldn't escape. I
was trapped!

CHARLOTTE MCGREAVY (11)

Soham Village College

THE RIDE

I was whizzing; it stopped. I stepped out. My
knees were wobbling. I felt sick and dizzy. I clung
to my Dad. I was afraid, didn't want to go near it.
My brain was still spinning. I started crying.
We drove away. Soon I would be home.

ALEX LOWE (11)

Soham Village College

TRAPPED

I'd begged my mum not to leave me. It was a
bright summer's day. However, something had
made it seem like a dull, rainy day. I walked slowly
towards it, not knowing what to do. I walked in
but never came back out of the … *new school*.

CHLOE GIMBLETT (11)

Soham Village College

FEAR ...

It was taking me higher, the water beneath my feet. Was it going to drop me? The sun tore down and burned the back of my neck. Sweat and despair trickled down my face. I tried to stop crying as it was taking me higher ... on the London Eye.

FRANCESCA HAGUE (11)

Soham Village College

INFORMATION

We hope you have enjoyed reading this book - and that you will continue to enjoy it in the coming years.

If you like reading and writing, drop us a line or give us a call and we'll send you a free information pack. Alternatively visit our website at www.youngwriters.co.uk

Write to:
Young Writers Information,
Remus House,
Coltsfoot Drive,
Peterborough,
PE2 9JX

Tel: (01733) 890066
Email: youngwriters@forwardpress.co.uk